Little One

Story Keeper Series
Book 12

Dave and Pat Sargent (*left*) are longtime residents of Prairie Grove, Arkansas. Dave, a fourth-generation dairy farmer, began writing in early December 1990. Pat, a former teacher, began writing in the fourth grade. They enjoy the outdoors and have a real love for animals.

Sue Rogers (*right*) returned to her beloved Mississippi after retirement. She shared books with children for more than thirty years. These stories fulfill a dream of writing books—to continue the sharing.

Little One

Story Keeper Series
Book 12

By Dave and Pat Sargent
and Sue Rogers

Beyond "The End"
By Sue Rogers

Illustrated by Jane Lenoir

Ozark Publishing, Inc.
P.O. Box 228
Prairie Grove, AR 72753

Cataloging-in-Publication Data

Sargent, Dave, 1941–
    Little One / by Dave and Pat Sargent
and Sue Rogers ; illustrated by Jane Lenoir.—
Prairie Grove, AR : Ozark Publishing, c2004.
        p. cm. (Story keeper series ; 12)

        "Be inventive"—Cover.
        SUMMARY: A little Cherokee girl wanted
to be big. Her wise mother guided her to do
things she was old enough to do well, until...
        ISBN 1-56763-925-9 (hc)
                1-56763-926-7 (pbk)

        1. Indians of North America—Juvenile
fiction. 2. Cherokee Indians—Juvenile fiction.
[1. Native Americans—United States—Fiction.
2. Cherokee Indians—Fiction.] I. Sargent, Pat,
1936– II. Rogers, Sue, 1933– III. Lenoir, Jane,
1950– ill. IV. Title. V. Series.

        PZ7.S243Li 2004
        [Fic]—dc21   2003090098

Copyright © 2004 by Dave and Pat Sargent
and Sue Rogers
All rights reserved

Printed in the United States of America

Inspired by
those who treat nature,
all creation, with respect.

Dedicated to
all who have Indian blood
running through their veins.

"Indian blood is like gold.
No matter how thinly spun,
it shines just as bright."
Anonymous

Foreword
Adsila, called Little One, is a young Cherokee girl who wants to be big enough to do all the things her sisters do. Her grandmother is very wise. She asks Adsila to find a dirt dauber nest. It is important—very important. Adsila has to think. She has to be brave.

Contents

If you would like to have the authors of the Story Keepers Series visit your school, free of charge, just call us at 1-800-321-5671 or 1-800-960-3876.

One

A Wigwam of Sisters

The Great Spirit gave us our land. It is beautiful, bountiful land. Trees, shrubs, and herbs are plentiful. Many birds nest in the trees. The mountains are filled with animals. They splash the sky with color and fill the air with song. Lakes and rivers are cool and clear and full of fish. It is a good land.

The forest and river supplied things to build our shelter. My father built the main house from hickory poles and long stiff cane plant stems covered with a mixture of clay and

1

grass. My mother and sisters cut the grass.

"I will collect clay from the riverbank," I said.

"No, Little One. Many moons will pass before you are old enough," said my mother. "But you are just right to mix the grass and clay."

This was a good job. I could walk up and down in the mud. It squished between my toes. It tickled. It was cool.

I began to think, "What would happen if...I wonder...Yes!" Up in the air I jumped. Flat on my back I splashed. Down in the clay I sank. Building a wigwam was fun!

My father cut large pieces of chestnut bark for the roof. We will be safe and dry.

A wigwam makes a comfortable summerhouse. There is room for my mother, my father, my grandmother, an aunt, my four sisters, and me. My name is Adsila, meaning "blossom."

Wigwams are cold in the winter. Father built a smaller round house for sleeping in cold weather. It was low and partly underground. He made a cone-shaped roof of poles covered with earth. Inside were beds and a fire pit. It was smoky but warm.

My father cleared trees to make room for crops. My mother grew corn, squash, sweet potatoes, and beans. My father also hunted deer, bear, and small game with his bow and arrow, spear, and blowgun.

My father worked hard to feed, clothe, and shelter a family of eight women and himself. His canoe was old. He needed a new one!

My father decided it was time my oldest sister married. That would bring another man to the wigwam.

It was Green Corn Moon. My Cherokee people grew three kinds of corn. One was eaten roasted in the coals of our fires. Another was boiled with vegetables. One was ground to make corn bread. Tassels were now showing on the corn in my mother's field. It was time for the Green Corn Ceremony! We would have four days of celebrating the ending of the old year and the beginning of the new.

"It is time our Tayanita took a husband," my father said to my mother and Grand Ma. "She is a beautiful girl and she needs a fine husband."

"Yes," my mother agreed. "We will look for a fine young warrior at the Green Corn Ceremony."

Grand Ma's eyes danced with delight. She had noticed Tayanita watching a handsome warrior at the ceremonial grounds when the First New Moon of Spring Ceremony was celebrated. Tayanita had shared fruits with him. She had blushed when he smiled at her.

"He must be a good hunter," my father added. "Ask if he can build a canoe."

Two

The Green Corn Ceremony

The ceremonial grounds are crowded. Every side of the square ground is filled. The women and girls are wearing their best dresses. My dress is made from woven fibers found in the bark of young mulberry saplings.

"Mama," I asked, "am I pretty enough to dance in the stomp dance tonight?"

"My Little One," answered my mother, "you are pretty enough to be the head shaker, but you are too young. Many moons from now you will wear the turtle shell shakers and lead the dance. But tonight you are just right to listen to the wonderful Story Keepers."

A Sacred Fire is in the middle of the square. The song leader dances out. The head shaker follows.

The others join in. They form a
spiral of dancers. They dance around
the fire.

The dancers' hearts and left hands are toward the fire. The step is a slow shuffling stomp of the feet, one after the other.

"Look, Mama. Look! Tayanita is dancing," I whispered. "Who is the handsome warrior before her?"

"He is from the Wolf Clan. I know his mother," she answered. There was a sparkle in her eye I had never noticed.

After the stomp dance comes the feather dance. And after the feather dance is the buffalo dance. Sometime during the night there will be a snake dance.

The best part is when my father and mother dance.

Many rituals fill the four-day celebration. Many games such as A-ne-tsa (Stickball) and Tsung-sy'unvi (Marble Game) are played. We feast on fry bread and special foods. The Story Keepers share the stories and legends of our people.

I love to hear "How Turtle's Back Was Cracked." When persimmons are ripe, we remember when Possum and Turtle were best friends. Possum could climb a persimmon tree; turtle could not. Possum would take careful aim and drop the fruit into Turtle's mouth, the story goes.

One day a wolf leaped into the air and snatched the persimmons before they got to Turtle's mouth. Turtle did not even see the big wolf. It was Possum who had to stop him.

Somehow Turtle's bragging about teaching the wolf a good lesson turned into him thinking he alone had slain the wolf. He decided it was his right to take a tribute from the dead wolf, so he cut off the wolf's ears. He fixed them onto two long wooden sticks to make wolf-ear spoons.

Turtle took his wolf-ear spoons and went visiting. It was the custom to offer a visitor some thick corn soup. Soon everyone was talking about what a mighty hunter Turtle must be if he ate corn soup with wolf-ear spoons, the story continues.

Word got back to the rest of the wolves. They were angry. This was a terrible insult. The wolves decided to do something about it.

That's all I know so far. I want to hear the Story Keeper finish this story so I will learn what happened to Turtle. I want to learn why you never see a turtle eating corn soup with a wolf-ear spoon.

"Mama, you were right. The stories are just right for me. I am a good listener. I learned not to brag. I learned the colors of the directions.

But I did not learn who the warrior is."

"You are learning fast, Adsila," said my mother. "The warrior is Dustu. He and Tayanita will soon be married. He will live in our family."

"But, Mama, can he build a canoe?" I asked.

"Yes, my child," answered my mother. "Dustu can build a canoe. And he can build wigwams. He is a good hunter and he is very brave. Just like your father!"

Three

Flower Moon

Tayanita and Dustu got married at the beginning of Fruit Moon. Grand Ma made her a beautiful pair of white moccasins decorated with quillwork and fringe.

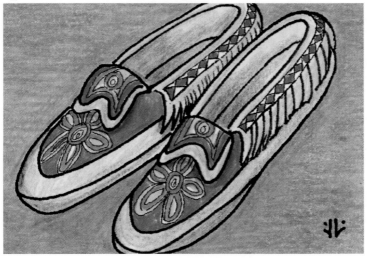

Aunt Leucreta gathered honey-suckle and made her gift basket. Tayanita and my mother were busy making her dress.

I looked all around. Everyone was busy. I began to cry.

"What is wrong, Little One?" my mother asked.

"I am too little to do anything," I sobbed.

"Oh no. You are just right to choose the wedding gift on the day of the wedding. It must be the largest ear of ripe corn in our field. It is to go in the gift basket for Tayanita's gift to her new husband. It will show that she is willing to be a good Cherokee wife. Will you do that?" asked my mother.

"Yes! Thank you, Mama. I will go now and check each ear of corn in the field. Tayanita, you shall have the finest ear of corn Mother Earth has ever grown," I cried.

When the wedding day arrived, Dustu and Tayanita met in the very center of the council house by the Sacred Fire. The priest blessed the fire and the union of the two. He asked for a long and happy life for them.

The groom gave the bride a ham of venison to show his intention to always keep meat in their household. Tayanita gave him the fine ear of corn! The wedding party danced and feasted for hours.

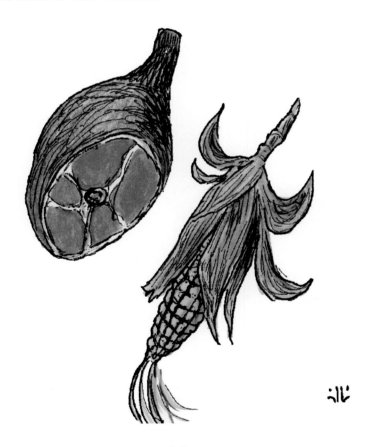

Much time has passed, and now, it is Flower Moon. Tayanita has a new baby boy!

Grand Ma and I gathered a big basket of cattails from a marsh near the river.

"We will need plenty for our Little One," Grand Ma said.

Little One had been asleep in his cradleboard on Grand Ma's back. He woke up crying. Grand Ma showed me how to pull the cattails apart. They made a basket of fluff. She took Little One out of the cradleboard. We knew why he was crying! Grand Ma let me take the cradleboard outside and empty the soiled fluff. I hurried back inside. We filled the cradleboard with clean fluff. Little One was still crying.

"Bring some powder, Adsila," Grand Ma said. I found the powder cloth. There was no powder left! Little One cried louder.

"How is the powder made, Grand Ma?" I asked.

"From dirt dauber nests," she

said. "But your father gathered all he could find."

Little One was howling now!

I tried to think. I had watched dirt daubers down by the river. They rolled tiny balls of clay and flew away. Where did they build their nests? It was out of the rain. It was a place my father did not go.

"Grand Ma, I will be back," I said. I grabbed a basket and a sharp-edge bone. I ran to the river. Large rocks jutted out over the banks of the river. I scooted down the path to the water's edge. I looked up. There they were—dirt dauber nests on the underside of rocks. Some were very high. Some were lower. But none were low enough for me to reach.

I looked for a way to get to the nests. Trees were growing near the rocks. I put the sharp bone in my mouth and the basket on my head. Up a tree I climbed.

When I got to the first big rock, I climbed out on it. Standing on it, I gathered a basket of big dirt dauber nests beneath the rock above.

Down I climbed. I could hear Little One still crying. Grand Ma was so happy to see the dirt dauber nests. She quickly broke one open. She scraped out the inside and put the dry nest in the powder cloth. She tied up the corners and pounded the cloth with a rock. And soon the nest was a fine powder.

"You must offer some of this to the four winds," Grand Ma said. She tossed pinches as she gave thanks.

She tied the cloth back together and then patted Little One's bottom. He went to sleep!

My grandmother said, "I will speak to your mother, Adsila. She must never call you Little One again. You are much too big for that name. Come with me and I will show you how to grind corn into meal. We will have corn bread with our vegetables tonight."

She handed me a wooden bowl and a long pointed stone. I felt big enough to grind corn for the whole village!

Four

Cherokee Facts

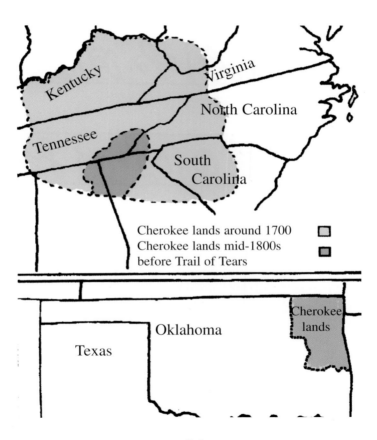

Cherokee lands around 1700
Cherokee lands mid-1800s
before Trail of Tears

Some of Sequoyah's syllabary written in his own hand.

Sequoyah introduced the Cherokee alphabet in 1824.

There is one character for each of the 86 syllables of the tribal tongue.

Stickball

Cherokee
Marbles

33

Summer house

Summer
arbor

Wattle and daub

Winter house

34

Early style

Square
bottom

Later style

Burden baskets

Round
bottoms

Covered basket

Woman with
burden basket

35

Cherokee
beadwork,
Mississippian design

Cherokee
beadwork

Cherokee
beadwork

Cherokee
beadwork

Cherokee
beadwork,
traditional 4 winds

Beyond "The End"

LANGUAGE LINKS

● The spoken language of the Cherokee has a soft flowing sound. Learn to say "hello" in Cherokee. Also learn to spell and say your name in Cherokee. See <www.ipl.org/div/ kidspace/hello/cherokee.html>. There are 22,500 people in our country who speak Cherokee. Now you can say "hello" to 22,500 people and tell them your name! (You can also learn the Cherokee numerals here.)

CURRICULUM CONNECTIONS

● Native Americans did not hire contractors to build their homes, or order lumber, nails, and shingles from the building supply store. They used natural resources for all their needs. Adsila helped to build her family's home. Discover what kind of houses Native Americans built in the Northeast, in the deserts of the Southwest, and in the Great Plains.

● In which cultural group did the Cherokee tribe belong?

● In what state do most of the Cherokee live today? If you and your family moved to another state, how would you travel? Read about the Cherokees' journey to their new state.

● The Cherokee year is divided into 12 periods, like our months. They call their months "moons" and have names for each moon. See <www.telliquah.com/moons.htm>. My birth moon is called "Cold Moon." In which month was I born? What is your birth moon?

● Visit the official site of the Cherokee Nation: <www.cherokee.org>.

THE ARTS

● Before Grand Ma used the powder she made from the dirt dauber nests, she gave thanks and tossed a pinch of the powder toward the east, north, west, and south. Each direction has a symbolic color to the Cherokee: red is for east–symbolic of success or triumph; blue is for north–symbolic of failure or trouble; black is for west–symbolic of death; and white is for south–symbolic of peace and happiness.

● Draw a picture of a war club, the soul of an enemy, a man who is a failure, and a love charm. Think of what each picture represents. Select the symbolic color for each of the pictures.

GATHERING INFORMATION

● Who was Sequoyah? What important contribution did he make to his people, the Cherokee? He called it "Talking Leaves."

● Find the answer to these questions in an encyclopedia. There can be several volumes in an encyclopedia set. Where do you begin? First decide what word tells the main point. Is it the name of the person? (Use the "S" volume to look up *Sequoyah.*) Is it the name of the tribe? (Use the "C" volume to look up *Cherokee.*) Or is it the name of the contribution? (Use the "T" volume to look up *Talking Leaves.*)

● See who finds the two answers first—GO!

THE BEST I CAN BE

● The American Indians strongly believed and taught their children that the Great Spirit dwells in every object, in every person, and in every place. They were very careful to give thanks for the bounty of the earth and to never take more than needed.

● This practice is exemplified in Adsila's story in an unusual way. She and her friends had seen the dirt dauber nests every time they went swimming, yet they had not disturbed them. Now they were needed!

● Though you may still be young, like Adsila, you are just right to learn to be kind to our earth and all living things. Make a list of things you can do to protect our earth.